DATE DUE			

16054

F
KRO

Kropp, Paul.

Runaway

PAUL KROPP

RUN-AWAY

Editorial development and production: Sandra Gulland
Design: Artplus/Brant Cowie
Illustrations: Heather Collins

EMC Publishing, St. Paul, Minnesota

Library of Congress Cataloging in Publication Data

Kropp, Paul
  Runaway.

  (Encounters series)
  Summary: Abused by her alcoholic father, Kathy runs away to her gra
parents. She eventually comes to realize that her reformed father needs l
rather than censure.
  [I. Alcoholism—Fiction. 2. Child abuse—Fiction. 3. Family problen
Fiction. 4. Runaways—Fiction] I. Collins, Heather, ill. II. Title. III. Ser
Kropp, Paul. Encounters series.

PZ7.K93Ru   [Fic]   81-5356
ISBN 0-88436-822-X   AACR2

Encounters Series Titles:

Burn Out	Fair Play
Dead On	Hot Cars
Dirt Bike	No Way
Dope Deal	Runaway

Published by EMC Publishing
180 East Sixth Street
Saint Paul, Minnesota 55101

Printed in the United States of America
0 9 8 7 6 5 4 3 2 1

CONTENTS

CHAPTER

Some days are so rotten you just wish you were born a goldfish. I mean, what does a goldfish do besides swim around inside a bowl all day? Does a goldfish have to put up with parents? Does a goldfish have a boyfriend who promises the world but can't come up with a subway token? Does a goldfish ever try to leave its bowl and go live on a shag rug?

No. Goldfish are a lot smarter than people. I wonder if they ever stare out the glass bowl and figure out how much better off they are than humans.

My friend Tracy thinks I'm joking

when I tell her I want to be Kathy the goldfish. She thinks it's one of the jokes I tell to hide from all the rotten things happening to Kathy the human being. Maybe she's right.

I was lucky that Tracy walked home with me on Thursday. It put me in a good mood by the time we got to my apartment. Tracy was moaning and groaning about a lot of stuff—nobody asks her out, her parents are too strict, she's too fat. I always tell her that she's better off than I am. I've been going out with Peter for almost a year and he just causes problems. If she thinks her parents are strict, she should just see my father. He makes King Kong seem like a nice guy. She hates being fat, but all I can say for being skinny is that you get nicknames like "Toothpick." Even my grandfather calls me "Toothpick" and sometimes I think he's the only real friend I have.

I said goodbye to Tracy and took the elevator up to our floor. Until I left the elevator, I didn't know there would be any trouble. Then I could hear my father's voice from out in the hall.

"When I say do the dishes, I mean do the dishes. Don't just stare at me, get moving!"

I couldn't hear what my sister said back. She's only eleven and can't yell nearly as loud as he can. But there was no problem hearing my father screaming at her.

"I said, get moving!"

When he started swearing, I knew what would happen next, so I started running down the hall. I fumbled around in my purse looking for the keys.

I heard the first slap before I got the door open. I heard another one after I got inside and ran for the kitchen.

With one quick look I saw what was happening. My little sister, Shelley, was crying her eyes out over in the corner next to the garbage can. She was curled up in a ball to keep my father from hurting her too badly. My father was ready to hit her again when he spun around and saw me. He was red in the face and smelled like he was drunk.

"Keep your hands off her," I yelled at him. Then I put myself between him and Shelley and stared right at him.

"Stop it," I yelled.

He raised his hand as though he was going to hit me, too. Then he let it drop. He looked like some overgrown little kid who had just lost his rubber ducky.

We all stood there, frozen, for about a minute. Nobody seemed to know what to do next, so I gave my father an order.

"I think you should go lie down."

He nodded and went off toward the bedroom. I got Shelley a Kleenex from the bathroom and helped her up. By the time we got to the living room, we could hear my father snoring away in his bed.

"What happened?" I asked.

"It was awful, Kathy. I got home from school a little early because it was a sports day. As soon as I came in I could see that Old Grizzly was in one of his moods."

"Old Grizzly" was the name we used for our father, but we never said it to his face.

"Drinking?"

"Yeah, people could probably smell it all the way down the hall. So I come in and sit down and I was going to start my homework."

I didn't believe that so I gave Shelley
a look.

"O.K., so I was just sitting down doing
nothing and he comes in screaming. I go
out to the kitchen and there's nothing in
the sink but the dishes from breakfast.
So I tell him the dishes aren't worth the
trouble and he throws a fit."

"You should know better than to say
something like that when he's drunk."

"Are you going to tell me it's my
fault?" Shelley said sharply. Then she
started to breathe funny and I knew she
was going to cry. I hugged her.

11

"I'm sorry, Shelley, I didn't mean that. It's just that the smallest thing sets him off when he's been drinking. So you've got to be careful, extra careful when the two of you are alone here."

I looked down at Shelley and really felt sorry for her. For some reason, my father had always been a lot harder on her than he was on me. Shelley often said that I was the "favorite" and she was right. Ever since I can remember, it was Shelley who got in trouble even when I deserved it.

It wasn't fair, really. She was still so small and she had always been thinner than me. Maybe that's why my father picked on her. Shelley was always wearing long-sleeved sweaters to cover the bruises on her arms. At school she found excuses not to take gym. She said she was sick or something, but really she didn't want anyone to see the bruises.

Some kids, like my friend Tracy, *say* that their parents treat them rough. But if they can talk about it, you know it's not that bad. I bet Shelley never told anyone that our father just went crazy beating her up.

"Come on, cheer up," I said. "He leaves for work at five so maybe we can go out and do something later."

Shelley stopped crying and looked up at me. "You mean you'll take me roller-skating?"

I groaned. I was about as good on roller skates as a moose trying to disco dance. But my mother wouldn't let Shelley go alone, and she was so crazy about it that I had to give in.

"I guess so," I grunted.

CHAPTER

I wasn't in a good mood when I went off to school the next day. My classes didn't make me feel any better. In history, the teacher asked me to tell the class about Sir John A. Macdonald. I said he was Ronald McDonald's brother and he made the first Big Mac. Everyone laughed except the teacher—he just shook his head and told me to write out a half page from the book. Some people have no sense of humor.

I was sitting alone in the lunchroom when I saw Tracy coming toward me. She had her lunch bag in one hand and four bags of potato chips in the other. The chips are what make her so fat. She told me once that she had tried to stop eating potato chips. She went without them for almost four days. Then she started to get potato-chip fits and would sneak down to the grocery store to buy some.

"Didn't you know anything about Sir John A. Macdonald?" she asked me.

"Of course I did! I know all about Macdonald and 1867 and all that. I just thought the class was a bore and you guys could use a joke."

"Oh," she said, "is that why you're in such a rotten mood?"

"No."

"Oh."

We just sat there for a minute and didn't say anything. Tracy opened up some potato chips and started eating.

"So what's the problem?" she asked with her mouth full.

I didn't really know whether I wanted to talk to Tracy or not. A lot of things had been getting me down—Peter, school, my father, just living in Skokie. I had talked about some of these things to Tracy, but she was pretty useless when you had a problem because she had so many of her own.

On the other hand, who else was there?

"My father was beating Shelley again last night," I said.

"He's sick," Tracy answered.

That was Tracy's answer to almost everything. If a guy tried to make out with you, or a friend chewed his fingernails, or your sister collected stamps—Tracy would always say they were sick.

"Tracy, if you had your way, half the people in Chicago would be locked up in the hospital. My father is not sick. He may be a bit too strict, a little old-fashioned, but he's not sick."

"I mean it, Kathy. We had a health class about child abuse where they had some people in from Children's Aid. I kept on thinking about your dad."

"Hey, you ask me to talk to you about a problem and the next thing you do is say my father should be locked up for child abuse. Cut it out!"

"I didn't say he should be locked up. He just needs some sort of help. Maybe he can't understand why you act the way you do. Or maybe he was beaten up when he was a kid, you never know. You remember when he broke Shelley's arm?"

"Yeah."

"The doctor could have done something then if only you had said what happened. Instead, you lied and covered up for your father and now you still have a problem."

Tracy was talking about the time, two years back, when my father really hurt Shelley. She had been talking back to him so he started hitting her pretty hard.

She fell backward and broke her arm. When we went to the hospital, the nurse asked how it happened. My mother and I said that Shelley had tripped on the stairs because we didn't want my father to get in trouble. The nurse shook her head as if she didn't believe us, but nobody asked us again.

"So it's all my fault?" I said.

"That's not what I was trying to say," Tracy said with a sigh.

"That's how it came out. Look, I am not my father's keeper. I do most of the work around the house now and I'm not going to play policeman, too."

"Don't get mad at me," Tracy said, eating her potato chips quicker than ever. "I just think you should talk to somebody at Children's Aid if you really want help."

"What I really want is to run away from here," I said, staring at Tracy.

She dropped her bag of potato chips.

"You're kidding."

I was sort of half kidding and half telling the truth. Whenever my father went crazy on us, I always thought about getting out of the house. I would think about setting up my own place in Los Angeles or maybe hitchhiking to Miami. I knew these plans were crazy, but I still thought about them. Lately, I had been thinking about them more and more.

"I don't know what I want right now. I just wish I was eighteen and school was finished and I could get out of the house. Or maybe Peter and I could, you know . . . ."

"Yeah, and you can get pregnant like Donna Wilson and go live in a housing project."

"Thanks a lot. Look, you can stuff your face with potato chips without me around. I've had enough."

I threw my lunch bag in the garbage and walked out of the lunchroom. I felt like pounding Tracy's potato chips into mush. She was always getting me mad like that. I'd start talking about a problem or an idea I had and she'd make the whole thing seem stupid.

I knew it was silly to dream about going off to live with Peter. I was only thinking out loud a little when Tracy started getting wild ideas. She must have some sort of hang-up about boys because all she can think of is getting pregnant.

I was thinking about more serious things. I only hoped Peter would be just as serious when he took me to the concert that night.

CHAPTER

The phone didn't stop ringing from the minute I got home from school—it was Tracy. I told my mother I didn't want to talk to her. My mother lied for me and told Tracy that I was out. Tracy kept phoning back every fifteen minutes to see if I had come home yet. It was driving me crazy.

Peter came to pick me up before I really went loony. I was just leaving with him when the phone rang again.

"What should I tell her now?" my mother asked.

"Tell her I was eaten by a kangaroo

that went strange," I said as we went out the door.

I could hear my mother mumbling as we walked down the hall to the elevator. Sometimes my mother is so weak it really gets to me. She's the sort of person who goes into a panic if you ask her what the weather is like outside. She couldn't talk back to me or my father and probably couldn't even lie to Tracy. I figured she'd just tell Tracy the truth—that I didn't want to talk to her.

"What's the problem?" Peter asked.

"I had a fight with Tracy and don't want to see her. Let's talk about something else."

"Oh," Peter said, and then he shut up. There were a lot of great things about Peter. He was beautiful—great eyes, wide shoulders and a super bum. He was a beautiful person, too, really kind and gentle to me. Peter had left high school last year and gotten a job at a drafting company. He figured if he wanted to move up he would have to go to Oak Park. So he was saving his money and making plans for next year.

Peter only had one problem—he didn't

like to talk. Since he was going out with me that wasn't too big a problem. I can talk and joke around enough for two people. But sometimes I wished he would say a little more. Like when we're waiting for the elevator and all we can hear is my mother mumbling.

Peter had one other problem which came up as soon as we got on the elevator.

"Hey, come on," he said, pulling me toward him.

"Would you just wait a while. This is an elevator and anyone could get on it, you know."

He gave me a look like he was three years old and I had just stolen his best toy. I gave in and we started fooling around.

I should have known better than to start doing that in the elevator. It stopped on the fifth floor and the superintendent got on. He stared at the two of us and I turned red.

It takes a long time to get down to Lincoln Park by bus or train. Peter was saving his money for next year so he didn't have a car. I didn't mind the long trip much because I had a lot to talk about.

Peter listens really well. Some people will tell you what to do or ask stupid questions. Peter just sits there and nods his head. I told him about my father hitting Shelley and how I had to stop him. I talked about going to the Children's Aid and said that I didn't want to. Peter listened to everything and hardly said a word.

"Let's go over to the new sports center," I said when we got to Lincoln Park.

"Sure," Peter said.

We ran along the paths that led to the kid's part of the park. Peter bought me a hot dog and then we ran inside.

We came to these big punching bags that hang down from the roof. There must be fifty of them hanging there, so big and close together you can get lost among them. I started hiding from Peter. I was still eating my hot dog when he bounced into the punching bags trying to find me. Finally, he did.

"Yecch," I yelled.

"What happened?" Peter asked,

pushing aside the punching bag between us.

"You pushed that thing at me and squashed my hot dog all over my face."

"I'm sorry," he said while I wiped the mustard off my nose. I could tell by the look in his eyes that he really was sorry. That's one of the things I love about him. He's like a little kid who can never hide anything he feels.

We played around at the sports center for about an hour. I laughed so much that my stomach began to hurt. Peter said we should go over to the open-air concert before I got sick.

All the real seats were filled by the time we got there. We had to sit up on the grass way back from the stage. I didn't mind sitting on the lawn, but I knew Peter would want to fool around as soon as it got dark. I just didn't feel like fooling around.

"Peter," I said as he put his arm around me.

"Uh-huh."

"Did you ever think about leaving home and going off to live by yourself?"

"Yeah."

"Well, why didn't you do it?"

"I guess because my parents are pretty good to me and I'd rather use my money for other stuff. Like taking you out to concerts," he said with a laugh.

"But what would you do if your parents were like mine? You know, there are times when I don't think I can stand to go back to my place any more. My father goes crazy and my mother can't seem to do anything about it."

"I think I'd stay put at least until I finished high school. It's only since I've been working that I figured out what use school is."

I thought that was a pretty dumb answer, the sort of thing my mother would say to me. I pulled out from under Peter's arm and slid away from him.

Peter moved over next to me again. He put his arm around me and started moving in close. That made me mad. I was trying to talk about a problem and all he could think about was fooling around. Sometimes I wonder if guys have sex on the brain all the time.

"Hey, come on," he said, reaching over.

"Tracy says I should get pregnant or married so I can leave home," I lied.

Peter just stared at me. I knew he wouldn't be ready for that one. The idea turned him off and he sat back away from me.

"That's pretty stupid," Peter said.

"I think so too."

"You've almost finished grade eleven, so all you have to do is hang in for another year and you can move out. You're not really ready to get married yet."

"Are you?" I asked him.

"Not yet. Give me about three years," Peter answered.

I stared at him for a minute and then gave him the kiss he wanted. The concert started up and I settled back on the grass in his arms. I listened to the music and started thinking about Peter and me. I tried to forget my problems at home, hoping they would go away. They didn't. They were getting ready for another attack.

CHAPTER

My father was waiting for me as soon as I got in the door. I wasn't too surprised because he had done it many times before. Peter and I always said goodnight down in the lobby because I knew my father might be waiting upstairs.

He had been drinking. I could smell the whisky as soon as I got in the apartment. Watching my father try to walk from the living room I knew for sure that he was drunk.

"You're late," he said.

I tried to figure out how I should answer. I wasn't really late. I had to be in by 1:00 and I still had fifteen minutes to go. Besides, I had told my mother we were going to Lincoln Park and that I might be a little late getting home.

On the other hand, when my father was drunk there was no sense getting him angry. I figured the smartest thing was to give in.

"Sorry," I said.

"I bet you're sorry. Out there necking with that freak you call a boyfriend. I won't have any girl of mine acting like that."

"Oh, cut it out," I said and walked past him into the kitchen. I thought maybe he would leave me alone if I got out of his way. I had already fought with Tracy and didn't want another fight with my father.

My idea didn't work.

"Katherine, don't you dare walk away when I'm trying to talk to you. You stay out all night and then you don't even listen to your parents. That's the problem with all you kids—you think you can do just what you want and not listen to anybody."

I stared at him. I figured if I couldn't

walk away from the fight I could try the silent act.

"Not only do you stay out all night but you have this crazy girl calling up on the phone all the time. How am I supposed to get any sleep around here with the phone ringing every time I turn around? Answer me, will you?"

He took hold of my arm and started to shake it. I pulled my arm away and backed into a corner of the kitchen. I think I started to get mad when he grabbed my arm.

"I'll give you a couple of answers if that's what you really want," I said. "I am not late and I have not been out all night. I got here at least fifteen minutes before you wanted me home and I came all the way across Chicago to do it. Why don't you give me a little credit instead of nagging me all the time?"

"Don't you raise your voice to me, young lady. You're just lucky that freak got you back here early or you'd be grounded for a month. You're lucky I even let you go out with somebody like that."

"Peter is not a freak. He's never been

drunk a day in his life and doesn't even take aspirin. You know what? Peter is going to do something with his life. He's going to be a success—not like you. He's not going to end up a lousy drunk who beats on little kids."

As soon as I said all that I knew I should never had said anything. My father started breathing funny and he looked like he was going crazy. He came over and grabbed both of my arms, shaking me.

My father is a trucker and has a lot of power in his arms. I began to understand

just how much power when he shook me. It was enough to scare me.

"Let go of me."

"Don't you ever say something like that to me."

"Let go," I yelled.

"You kids think you can just say anything you want to your parents, whatever garbage you have in your head. You'll show some respect to me, you hear, some respect!"

I heard my mother getting out of bed and that made me feel better. I figured my father couldn't do too much with her watching. I started to relax a little and then I made another mistake.

"I'll show you some respect as soon as you deserve it," I said.

He raised his arm high over his shoulder and slammed his fist into me. He hit me hard in the chest. Then he slapped my face with his hand.

I fell down on the floor, crying from the pain, and he stopped hitting me. Maybe the crying was enough to cool his anger or maybe it was my falling on the floor. He seemed to be standing over me, frozen, like some sort of statue.

My mother came in the room and my father drew back from me. He walked into the living room as if he was in a daze while my mother came over to me. She had a blank look on her face. She had seen fights like this too many times to get upset.

"Leave me alone," I yelled at her. I got up by myself and ran to Shelley's bedroom. Then I fell on her bed, sobbing.

"Kathy, it's all right. It'll all be over with in the morning," Shelley said. I could hear Shelley's words trying to calm me while my mother was saying something to my father in the other room.

A minute later there was a knock at the bedroom door.

"Yeah," Shelley called out as we got closer together on the bed.

"Kathy, I'm sorry," my father said, very quietly. He sounded like he was beaten worse than I was, like he was really sorry.

I kept quiet. I was still too upset, too scared and too angry to say anything that would make sense.

Shelley and I shared her bed that night. We stayed together half because I didn't want to be alone and half because we were afraid of what my father might do next.

CHAPTER

"I've got to get out of there," I told Tracy on Monday. "If Old Grizzly thinks he can just beat on me and get away with it, he'd better think twice."

"I don't blame you," Tracy said while chewing a potato chip.

I had taken the whole weekend to think over what had happened. It was partly my fault and I could see that. If I hadn't lost my cool and started pushing him, he would never have hit me.

But the whole thing was sick. I still had a bruise on my chest where he had hit me and my arms were black-and-blue.

And I hadn't even done anything wrong! I wasn't out late—I came home early. Peter wasn't a freak—he was so straight it wasn't funny.

"I'm just sorry I got you in so much trouble," Tracy said.

"To tell you the truth, I'm glad that somebody worries enough about me to call the house. If my parents would worry like that I wouldn't be leaving home."

"What are you going to do?" Tracy asked.

"I'm going to leave home and go live downtown with my grandfather. I called him last night and told him what happened. He said I could stay with him and grandma as long as I want."

"But what about school?"

"There's only a week to go here so I won't blow the year if I miss it. Maybe I'll take next year off or go to school downtown. The only thing I know for sure is that I've got to get out of that apartment before he kills me."

"I think you're getting too upset about this whole thing. Your father came back and said he was sorry," Tracy pointed out.

"All the sorry in the world won't fix a broken arm, you know."

Tracy didn't like the idea of my leaving home and some of her reasons made sense. But I figured the main reason she didn't want me to go was that she wouldn't have anyone to talk to.

I had spent a lot of time thinking out the whole problem. I figured my father needed something to shake him up, to make him see that he needed help. Besides, I wanted to show him that I could take care of myself. I'd get a job doing something so I could pay grandpa

room and board. Maybe I could move into my own apartment after a while.

When I got home after school I had to start packing. My mother wouldn't be home until six and my father was on a trucking run. That left me alone to pack up.

I was able to get a lot of clothes into a suitcase before Shelley came home from school. The clothes were easy to pack up—the problem was sorting out all the stuff I had saved up. I knew I couldn't take much with me, but I didn't want to leave everything behind.

"What are you doing?" Shelley asked as soon as she came in.

"Packing," I said.

"You're not going off with Peter, are you?" she asked.

"No, I'm going off to live by myself for a while. When Old Grizzly hit me last Friday, I finally decided to move out."

It took a little while for the words to sink in. I knew Shelley would be upset when I told her, so I had put it off to the last minute. Maybe I should have told her earlier to try to get her used to the idea.

"I wish I could leave too," Shelley said with a sigh.

"You're too young yet and he'd just send the police to get you back again," I explained.

"Kathy, can you tell me where you're going to go?"

I really didn't want to tell Shelley because I didn't know how much she could be trusted. The last thing I needed was my father coming after me.

"Come on, where are you going?" Shelley prodded.

"Promise you won't tell them, no matter what happens?"

Shelley nodded, looking much older and more serious than she was.

"Then I'll be at grandpa's if you want to get hold of me."

Shelley nodded and walked out of the bedroom. I couldn't hear what she was doing out in the living room and I didn't really want to know. It was hard enough packing up all my stuff without worrying about her crying as well.

I finally got the suitcase and a small book bag filled up. I took them out of the bedroom and set them in the hall by the doorway. Then I went back into the living room and found Shelley.

She was lying on the couch, her eyes red from crying. I sat down beside her and, for the first time, wondered if my decision was the right one. I thought about why I was doing it for a minute while I tried to make her feel better. The more I thought about it, the more I felt I was right.

"Kathy," she said, "if you stay here I'll take you roller-skating with the money I've got saved up. Really, I will."

She gave me a look that was so full of love, yet so hopeless, too, that I didn't know what to do.

"I can't, Shelley. I've made my decision and I have to stick by it. Besides, I told grandpa I was coming."

Shelley cried again, and though I tried not to, I was crying with her. There were still tears running down my face when I got on the elevator with all my stuff. I just wanted to get away and be alone for a while.

The elevator door opened and I saw the superintendent in the corner. I turned away from him and pressed "L."

"Going on a trip?" he asked.

"No, I'm jumping out of the bowl." I sucked in my cheeks and stuck out my lips to make a goldfish face in the corner of the elevator.

CHAPTER

My grandfather has got to be the greatest guy I've ever met. He lives downtown in this big, old house off Michigan. He's retired now and spends his time working on the three old Corvairs in the driveway, or playing songs on his fiddle, or telling wild stories about his days in the army. When I was a kid I used to love visiting him so I could hear him tell stories.

I rang the bell when I reached the house and waited for my grandfather to open the door. I was surprised to see my grandmother instead.

"Where's grandpa?" I asked.

"He's taking a nap, Kathy. He doesn't have quite as much strength as he did before the heart attack, you know."

I walked into the living room and sat down on an overstuffed couch. All the chairs and couches were overstuffed. Maybe that's why grandpa's house always seemed friendly, while my father's apartment seemed as nice as a dentist's office.

Grandpa came downstairs in five minutes or so. As soon as he saw me he broke into a smile.

"Kathy, it's so good to see you here. It's just a shame you had to come after your ... uh ... problem. I never will understand why Mina married that man."

"Grandpa, I'm going to go out looking for a job tomorrow so I'll be able to pay you room and board."

"Don't worry about that. Mom and I will be happy to take care of you for a while. Did I ever tell you about the time I left home?"

"No," I lied. He had told the story at least five times, but that was no reason not to hear it again.

"I was only thirteen but I wanted to prove I was a man, you know. So I went down to the army office in Bristol and told the major I wanted to sign up. He asked me how old I was so I lied and said sixteen. He said, 'Prove it.' I said I could swear better than any man he had. So he called for this other chap and we started cursing at each other. I think we kept on swearing for about three hours, if I remember right. When we were finally done, the major called the contest a draw. 'Any man who can swear like that should be in the army,' he said and signed me up right away."

"And you haven't said a single swear word since then," I said to finish the story.

"No reason to," grandpa answered. "Now get your suitcase up to the second bedroom and start unpacking. Dinner will be on the table before you know it."

Grandpa had given me a little room that had once been used by one of my mother's sisters. It still had the old wallpaper and there was a wooden bed along one wall. I looked out the window and could see the old water tower not too far away. For the first time in a week, I started to feel good again.

After I had unpacked, we sat down to dinner. My grandmother brought out a roast chicken, which looked great. She said she was sorry there were no potatoes but that grandpa shouldn't be eating them anyhow. That was enough to start grandpa going and he told a long story about a potato farmer he knew back in England.

After dinner I went up to my room and began to write a letter to Peter. I had not even finished the first page when I heard a noise downstairs. At first I thought it was the paper boy. Then I could hear that it was my father.

"Let me in," he said, pounding on the door. "I know Kathy's in there."

How could he find out, I asked myself. The only person who knew where to find me was Shelley—she must have told him everything.

"Calm down and let me unlock the door," my grandfather said.

"I know Kathy's here and you can't keep her from me."

"I wouldn't dream of keeping her from you, Vic," my grandfather said. "It's not my way to keep anybody anywhere."

My grandfather's voice was very quiet. He spoke as if he was talking to a little kid. "Quiet down and relax, Vic."

"Where is she? That's what I want to know. I want that girl home and I want her home tonight, you understand me? I'll get the police if I have to," my father shouted.

"You can call the police if you want, Vic, but it won't do any good. I don't want to explain the fine points of law to you but you don't have much of a case, you know."

I didn't know how much grandpa knew about the law, but I was glad he wasn't letting my father get at me. I knew the police wouldn't force you to go home if you were sixteen, but I didn't know what other rights my father might have.

"I know my rights and I want Kathy to come home," my father yelled.

"You shouldn't be so concerned about 'your rights,' Vic. Maybe you should spend some time making sure you're

doing the right thing for your family. I could tell you a funny story about that very thing. Why don't we just take a walk around the block and talk this whole thing over."

A minute later I could hear the door close. I ran to the window and peeked over the sill. The two men, my father and my grandfather, were walking down the street toward Michigan.

I didn't know what was going to happen. Even if the police wouldn't send me back, who could stop my father from *taking* me back? Grandpa wasn't strong enough to stop him and grandma and I couldn't do very much.

I really started to get scared. I couldn't tell what my father wanted. I didn't know if he'd been drinking and then beaten up Shelley to find out where I was. I didn't know what he might do to grandpa. A million thoughts went through my mind while I waited for them to come back.

The door opened. I could tell by the footsteps that only one person came in. I ran to the top of the stairs and looked down at the front hall—it was grandpa.

"What happened?" I asked him.

"We had a long talk about the problem and what he wanted. I told him a couple of stories to take his mind off things. After a while he calmed down and we agreed that you should stay here for a while."

I ran downstairs and gave grandpa a hug. "That's wonderful. That's the best news I've had in over two weeks."

"He really loves you very much, you know," my grandfather said. "He just doesn't know how to show it."

CHAPTER

A week later I had a job. It was a pretty awful job but the money wasn't bad. Grandpa said that the worst job he ever had was cleaning toilets for two weeks during the war. I told him that my job was feeding food to guys who spent their days cleaning toilets. The only good thing about my job was that I got a few laughs out of it.

I worked at Jan's Restaurant on Michigan, not far from my grandfather's house. I started work early in the morning. The old drunks who had been boozing all night were trying to sober up.

I served them coffee and made sure I got their money before they left the place. If they could sneak out before I got the money for coffee, I had to pay for it myself. I told my boss I didn't think that was fair. He just shrugged his shoulders and said, "This ain't the Ambassador."

After the drunks rolled out we got the young workers coming in for breakfast. These guys always paid their bill and often left big tips. What I didn't like was what they wanted for their tips. If my father had heard some of the gross things they said, he'd have punched out everybody in the place.

Then we could all sit around and rest a little before the lunch crowd came in. All the other girls working there seemed to be on the skids. Their men had left, or they'd quit school at age seven, or they'd popped one pill too many. There were only two men in the place—the dishwasher and my boss. Those two were the dumbest men I'd ever met. The dishwasher once asked me where I lived. I told him I was staying at the corner of Walk and Don't Walk. I think he really believed me.

After two days the place was starting to drive me crazy. I really couldn't talk to any of the people I worked with and I didn't want to talk to any of the customers. The crazy people who came in were starting to scare me, too. There was one guy who must have been on speed. When he came in, he shook up and down on the counter stool all the time he was eating. I kept on waiting for him to take off and fly away. Another guy came in every day and talked about the weather. He always said, "Nice day, wonderful day out," no matter what the weather was like. One day he came in soaking wet from the rain and said to me, "Nice day, wonderful day out." I wondered which of us was loony.

A week after I started at Jan's, I was sitting down before the lunch crowd came in, wondering how I could make it through the summer. Then I heard a voice behind me.

"Excuse me, miss."

I turned around and froze—it was Peter. I ran over and gave him a great big hug. I don't think I had ever missed anybody so much in my life.

"How'd you ever find out I was here?" I asked him.

"Your sister finally told me that I could find you at your grandfather's house. When I got there, he asked me who I was and then said you worked over here at the restaurant."

"I'm sorry, I was going to write you but this stupid job wears me out," I whispered.

"This place looks pretty awful. Can I get something to eat here that won't make me sick?"

"You're taking your chances—garbage on toast coming right up," I said.

I went off to get Peter a hamburger and fix myself up. The customers at Jan's were so awful that I always tried to make myself look as ugly as I could. Peter was a different story, though. I ran down to the washroom and did the best I could in a minute or so.

"Are you going to stay here all summer?" he asked when I got back.

"Why not?" I said. I may not have liked the restaurant very much, but that didn't mean I was going to give up and go home.

"It's awful."

"At least nobody beats me up."

"Oh, come on. I talked to your father on the phone last night and he sounds like he's really sorry. Maybe he's learned his lesson now and you could go back home," Peter said.

"My father talked to you? The last thing I heard was that you were a dope freak and I was lucky he even let me talk to you. You know, my father's got to be missing a few marbles upstairs. He's two different people—a nice, dull truck driver when he's sober, but a disgusting creep when he's drunk."

"Maybe you're being too hard on him."

"Too hard on him?" I started getting mad. "Are you two trying to talk me into coming home? I don't need anybody coming down here to tell me what a super guy my father is. I know the truth and I've got the bruises to back it up."

"Don't get angry at me," Peter said. He gave me the same kind of look he uses when I won't fool around with him.

"Don't give me that cute little-boy look and don't try to tell me what to do."

"I'm sorry I tried to tell you anything," he said. "It was a waste of a subway token even coming down here."

In a second he was up and out the door. I looked at him walking away and wanted to say something but I didn't know what. I wanted to go yell "I'm sorry," but I couldn't with everyone in the restaurant watching me. I just stood there.

"Kathy," my boss called out, "you've chased one customer away, now take care of the others, huh?"

I felt like throwing a cream pie in his face, but I knew he'd just take it out of my pay.

CHAPTER

Dear Peter,

I'm sorry. That's what I wanted to say when you went storming out of Jan's this morning. I didn't mean to make you angry and I really was glad to see you. I just can't seem to tell people out loud the way I really feel.

I've only missed two people since I came downtown, you and Shelley. That gives you some idea how important you are to me. I was so surprised when you came down to visit me that I didn't know what to say. Working at Jan's makes your brain turn into Jell-O.

I hate working there. My boss thinks a restaurant should be run like an army camp. Every time I blow my nose he tells me he'll take the Kleenex out of my pay. The other women who work there are like zombies. You remember that movie we saw about the zombies who walked around eating people? The whole bunch of them give me the creeps.

The customers are even worse. I swear that the next time someone gives me a pat on the rear I'm going to dump soup on his head. We had a guy come in last night who started throwing up all over. Then he left before paying for his coffee. Guess who had to clean up? And pay for the coffee?

I talked to Shelley on the phone last night and she says Old Grizzly (my father) has joined AA. Maybe you're right and he is trying to become more human. I want to wait at least a couple of weeks to see if he sticks with it.

My grandfather is in bed today. He hasn't been feeling very well for about a week and I can see that grandma is worried. Did he tell you any of his stories when you saw him? He has a great one about sneaking on a ship with a thousand nurses going to France. He won't tell me the whole story but I bet he'd tell it to you.

I'm not sure that I'm very happy here downtown. I like my grandparents a lot, but most of the other people I meet are pretty strange. It's funny how you can be in the center of millions of people and feel all alone.

I still think leaving home was a good idea and I'm not about to go back. It may be rough down here for a while, but I want to prove to myself that I can handle it.

I miss you and wish you'd come to see me again, or call me after three at my grandparents' house. I'm really sorry about being so dumb this morning. I didn't mean it.

Love,
Kathy

Dear Kathy,

How have you been since I called you? Are you still working at that awful restaurant on Michigan? Has Peter come down to see you yet?

I guess I had better stop all the questions and just get on with the letter before you think I've lost my marbles. I've been so upset about everything since you left that I'm eating even more potato chips. I've gained weight in the past two weeks and I feel like a blimp.

I talked to Shelley and she told me about your father joining AA. I think that's great and maybe it will help him a lot. I told Shelley that maybe she should join Alateen to find out what she can do to help your father. She said she might, but I know she'd do it if you pushed her a little.

Shelley seems to be taking things pretty well on her own. The only thing she said to me is that she can't go roller-skating any more. If that's her only problem I guess you shouldn't worry too much.

I've got to stop now and have some dinner. I'll finish this after.

Wow, I need chicken and gravy about as much as a hole in the head. In fact, I'd rather have the hole in the head. I'd weigh a lot less.

I saw your father this afternoon down at the grocery store and he looked awful. His skin is all white and he looks like he doesn't sleep any. Your mother looks about the same as always, which isn't saying much. I didn't talk to them very long and only about the price of hot dogs.

Remember that history teacher who always used to pick on you in class? We found out on the last day of school that he's not coming back next year. They say he got a job teaching in Alaska. At least he won't have any guys like me making jokes about Ronald McDonald.

It's too bad there aren't any decent guys down at Jan's. I can't believe the way you talk about your boss. You said that he won't go outside on windy days because the skin on his face flaps around so much. You've got to be kidding.

Things are really boring around here. Since you left I haven't had anybody to make me laugh or to make fun of me eating potato chips. It's no wonder I'm getting fat.

Maybe we could go out to a movie some day when you're not working. I still haven't got a job so I can get away any time. Give me a call and tell me what you think.

Yours,
Tracy

P.S. Shelley asked me to take her roller-skating but I was able to get out of it. I wish your mother would let her go out alone so she'd stop bothering both of us.

CHAPTER

I was reading Tracy's letter over for the second time when I heard my grandmother calling from downstairs.

"Kathy, Kathy come quick."

There was something about the sound of her voice that told me right away there was trouble. I ran out of my bedroom and bolted down the stairs as fast as I could.

As soon as I got to the living room I could see him. Grandpa was lying on the floor, his face white as a sheet. Grandma was next to him, holding him over on his side.

I looked at grandpa and saw that he was still breathing. Then I looked at my grandmother and tried to think of what to do.

"Call an ambulance, dear, and then bring me a blanket," she said, trying to keep calm.

She was right, of course. She seemed more in control of herself than I was. I ran out to the phone in the hall and tried to think of the number for an ambulance. My brain was a blank. I finally called the operator and asked for help.

There was a blanket in the closet near the front hall. I got it for my grandmother to put over grandpa and then went up to my room for more.

I know it only takes three minutes for an ambulance to get any place in Chicago. But when your grandfather seems almost about to die, it feels like hours. My grandmother and I didn't say much—we just waited.

After the ambulance came, things seemed to go much faster. They had grandpa on a rolling bed and out to the ambulance in maybe two minutes. Grandma got in with him and they raced off to the hospital. I was left behind with the police filling out a report. When we were done, they asked if I wanted a ride to the hospital, so I went with them.

My grandmother was in the waiting room when I got there.

"How is he?"

"He's resting now, the doctor says. They have to watch him quite closely because this is his second heart attack."

"Will he be all right?" I asked.

"We hope and pray that he will be, dear," my grandmother said. Then she grew quiet.

We had to sit in the waiting room for hours before we found out anything more. I hate hospitals. I've never even had an operation and I still hate hospitals. It may be because they smell like all the cleaning people went wild with Lysol spray. I'll never figure out how nurses can work in that smell all day long.

Grandpa's doctor finally came down the hall toward us. I tried to read his face before he said anything to see if the news was good or bad, but I couldn't.

"He's off the critical list, Mrs. Solway, and seems to be resting quietly now.

It's too early to say just how much long-term damage this has caused. We'll do some tests after Mr. Solway gets his strength back."

My grandmother just nodded and waited to hear more.

"If you'd like to be with him now, the nurse can take you down."

"Yes, yes, I'd like to be with him," my grandmother said as she got her coat. A second later she was walking down the hall with the nurse and I was left standing with the doctor.

"Doctor, what caused the heart attack?"

"It could be any number of things— old age, eating habits, stress, almost anything," he said.

"Would stress be like putting a person under a lot of pressure? I mean, making them do things they wouldn't do very often?"

"Sure. Sometimes any kind of change can put older people under stress. That's why travel or some new problem can bring on an attack. But there's no way you can pin down the cause of a heart attack to only one thing. I could explain

it to you better if you'd drop by the office, but right now . . . ."

"That's all right, doctor. Thanks very much for all you've done," I said.

The doctor went down the hall and I was left alone in the waiting room. It was a good thing because I started crying and I don't like people staring at me when I cry.

CHAPTER

I called up Jan's when I got home and said I was sick. Then I sat down on my bed and started thinking.

Grandpa was in the hospital and it was my fault. That was the first thing I said to myself. Then I tried to talk myself out of it—he's an old man, there are a lot of reasons for heart attacks, he really likes to have me around the house.

But I kept on seeing a picture of my grandfather with the blood rushing to his face when he talked to my father.

I fell back on the bed and tried to sort out my ideas. Peter was mad at me, my grandfather was in the hospital, my family wanted me to come home, my job was the pits. These things kept on running through my mind, like grooves on a record that you play over and over again. The more I thought about the whole thing, the worse I felt. I rolled over and started to think about being a gold-fish. How great it would be to swim around all day without any feelings, any troubles.

Downstairs, there was a knock at the door and I waited for my grandmother to answer it. Then I remembered she wasn't home, so I wiped my face and went down the stairs.

It was Peter and my sister, Shelley. I tried to think of something to say but couldn't find the right words. Instead, I put my arms around Shelley and gave her a hug.

"Got your letter," Peter said.

"Oh, Peter, I felt so bad about what happened at Jan's. It was all my fault, you know, just like everything else."

"How's grandpa?" Shelley broke in. "Grandma called the house and I asked Peter to bring me down."

"The doctor says he's going to live through it," I said. "They won't know about the long-term problems until next week."

We walked from the front door into the living room. Peter and I sat down on the couch and Shelley was about to sit on a chair across from us. Then she looked over at the two of us and waited.

"I think I'll make some tea," she said, leaving us to go to the kitchen.

I waited a second until she was out of the room and then I kissed Peter. "I feel so confused," I said. "Everything has been so strange since I left home that I can't even think straight. I don't have any idea what to do next."

"The last time I tried to give you advice was at Jan's and you had a fit. I'm almost afraid to say anything more," Peter answered.

"That was awful. I bit your head off just for telling me what I already knew. You were right—the restaurant is a dump."

"Maybe I was right about your father, too," Peter added.

"I don't know, I just don't know."

Shelley rolled out the tea pot on grandma's old tea wagon. She acted like she was a maid. Peter laughed when she said "One lump or two?" in a fake English voice. I waited until my tea was cool before I asked her what I really wanted to know.

"Shelley," I said, "has Old Grizzly changed any since I left?"

"Yeah, I think something really got to him, you know. After he talked to grandpa he seemed really changed. He walked around the apartment like a zombie for a while, but the big change was that he stopped drinking. I got home from school one day and there was no beer left in the fridge. The kitchen had a green garbage bag full of empty whisky bottles. I didn't know if he was on the worst drunk of all time or what until I saw him in the bedroom, calm as could be. He told me that he'd quit drinking and joined AA. I told him he was super."

"So he hasn't gone crazy since then, or gone back to drinking?" I asked.

"Not one slap, not one drink." Shelley rolled up the sleeves of her shirt. "Look, no marks or bruises anywhere."

I had to laugh at Shelley. She seemed really happy for the first time in years. She also seemed to have grown older in just the three weeks since I'd left.

"But he still wants you to come back home," Peter said. "What you really wanted when you left home was for your father to clean up his act. Well, he's trying. Now what are you going to do to give him some support?"

I was really confused. I knew Peter was right and that, in a lot of ways, I should go home. But a part of me didn't want to go back.

"But grandma may need some help around the house when grandpa comes home," I said.

"Kathy," Peter said, "that's just an excuse and you know it. Sure you can stay here for a while if your grandmother needs help, but what about the real decision?"

I looked over at Shelley to see if she could offer any help in the decision. She looked back at me for a second and then smiled.

"I still need somebody to take me roller-skating."

We all laughed. There was something really funny about the way Shelley boiled down a big decision into something as simple as roller-skating.

I looked back at Peter and knew that I had made up my mind. I felt like an awful weight had been taken off my chest.

"I'll go home," I whispered.

Shelley ran over and gave me a hug while Peter lay back on the couch smiling.

"But it's only because you want to go roller-skating," I laughed.

Books in this series:

BURN OUT
Bob and Chewie have a plan to catch the firebugs on Maple Street. The plan seems good at first. But when it backfires they get trapped in the basement of a burning house.

DEAD ON
What is making the strange sound in the hall outside Larry's room? It can't be a ghost. Larry does not believe in ghosts. But someone — or something — keeps leading him to the attic of the old house.

DIRT BIKE
Twenty cycles roar out of the start chute. Randy races toward the first turn on his yellow dirt bike. He looks over at Bozo and grits his teeth. Only one of them can come out the winner.

DOPE DEAL
Brian has to face a lot of problems. He gets busted by the cops, has to move back home and beats up his own brother. But his biggest problem comes when he takes on a whole motorcycle gang.

FAIR PLAY
When Andy Singh asks Carol to the party, she couldn't care less whether his skin is black or white. But her old boyfriend cares far too much. His jealousy and hate lead to a night of danger on the icy streets of Windsor.

HOT CARS
At first Robert doesn't know who is killing his dogs or wrecking his father's truck. When he gets trapped by a stolen-car gang, the answer almost kills him.

NO WAY
Pete only wants to show the others how brave he is. But his plan for the perfect rip-off falls apart. He ends up in trouble with the law. Now his old gang wants him to steal from the only people he really cares about.

RUNAWAY
Kathy wishes she were a goldfish. She has some good reasons — her father gets drunk and beats her, her best friend drives her crazy and her boyfriend wants to get too friendly. Will she be better off if she runs away?